Date Due

A VERY SPECIAL PET

A STORY PARADE PICTURE BOOK

A VERY SPECIAL PET

Story by LAVINIA DAVIS   *Pictures by* KURT WIESE

Publishers   GROSSET & DUNLAP   New York

IT BEGAN on a raw spring day when Jeff Manners rescued Blackie from the swamp and took him home. Jeff had been walking across the cold quiet fields when all of a sudden he heard the wild cawing and shrieking of the crows above the swamp. When he went down to see what it was all about, there was Blackie. The other crows flew off flapping and cawing, but Blackie stayed behind.

Blackie could neither caw nor flap, and when Jeff first found him he could hardly see. He just sat on a log in the very center of the swamp, with his head down and one bedraggled black wing hanging. Jeff never hesitated. He waded right into the swamp. Perhaps there were snakes around. Certainly there were snapping turtles. But Jeff thought of nothing but the pathetic bird on the log near the center of the swamp. He ruined a perfectly good pair of trousers going after Blackie. A month later his rubber boots still smelled like an assortment of dead fish, but he didn't care. He had rescued the crow.

Jeff brought Blackie home and fed him worms and grain. He made a warm, cozy nest for him in a box in his own room. When it was warm and sunny, he took him outdoors for an airing, and when it was especially cold and damp he draped an old bit of flannel around Blackie for a wrapper. With so much care, Blackie's wing and broken leg healed rapidly.

In gratitude, Blackie was a loyal pet. He was so loyal that he stuck to Jeff like a small black shadow.

But his loyalty wasn't very helpful for Jeff. It seemed as though he stuck close to Jeff just to bring him trouble.

It began when Blackie first followed Jeff to the dining-room table. Jeff sat down with the rest of his family and the first thing he knew Blackie was on his shoulder.

"Quite a pet, that crow," Jeff's father said, and Jeff beamed. But just at that minute Blackie decided to take a bath in Jeff's milk. Then Jeff upset the syrup pitcher, trying to stop him, and with that Jeff and Blackie were sent from the table.

Blackie made trouble again at the Sunday School picnic. He took one bite out of each of the strawberries on top of the beautiful shortcake that Mrs. Hamersby, the minister's wife, had made especially for the picnic.

"It'll be the same way at the pet show," Jeff's big sister Ellen said the morning the invitations arrived. "You'll take Blackie along, and he'll just get you into trouble."

In his heart Jeff agreed, but when Blackie came flapping onto his knee and looked at him with his one good eye, Jeff couldn't resist. Besides, Jeff didn't have any other pet. Ellen had her dog Ben and the big Persian cat, Emir. Even Jeff's little sister, Susy, had her own kitten, Fluffy Toes.

While the others were discussing the pet show, Blackie flapped up onto Jeff's shoulder. He rubbed his head against Jeff's neck just as though he knew what Jeff was thinking.

"Blackie's going in the special pet class," Jeff said firmly. "Even if he's bad, he's a very special pet."

The day of the pet show dawned cool and clear and perfect. It was one of those rare June days when any-

one from a pet crow to a great aunt would feel well, and Jeff was glad he had decided to take Blackie along. When he saw Ellen climb into the back seat of the station wagon with Ben and Emir, and Susy climb into the front seat with Fluffy Toes, he was gladder than ever. It would be awful to be the only one in the family who didn't have a pet to exhibit.

When Mother had driven them halfway to the pet show, Susy pulled out three very mangled packages from a paper bag. "I almost forgot!" she said. "I've made decorations for each of us."

Jeff shivered. He could just guess what Susy's decorations would be like. When the packages were opened, the decorations were even worse than Jeff had expected. The one for Ellen's pet was a regular ruff of orange and purple paper with greenish streaks in it where the paste had come through. It looked big enough for a tiger, but Susy was sure it was just the right size for Ben. Her own decoration was a braid of three colors of wool for Fluffy Toes' neck! Jeff opened his package very, very carefully, and then held his breath.

"It's a necklace for Blackie," Susy explained proudly, "because he likes shiny things."

It was a necklace all right and it *was* shiny! Susy had taken shoestring and a heavy needle and strung together six small tin can tops and about twenty pieces of a colored cardboard cereal box. They were not even cut-outs, Jeff realized, just odds and ends of jagged cardboard that she'd cut out any which way.

"It was hard to make," Susy said. "I had to hammer holes in the tin tops before I could string them."

Jeff nodded. It was all too plain from the litter of markings that dotted the tin covers how the holes had been made. Jeff struggled to be kind.

"Thanks a lot, Susy," he said. "It's—it's swell."

"Try it on," Susy insisted, and Jeff held it around Blackie's neck. Blackie was almost hidden. The tins were big enough for a crow's suit of armor and he looked snowed in behind the litter of colored paper.

"It's too big," said Susy unhappily, and her lower

lip was suddenly thick and shaky. "It's much too big."

Jeff was just wishing that Mother or Ellen or some-
one would say something when a terrible thing happened. Ellen had been fitting Ben's ruff around his
neck when all of a sudden it blew away.

"Oh!" said Ellen, but her voice didn't sound excited
a bit. "Oh, what a shame! It—it just blew away."

Jeff looked at his older sister through narrowed
eyes. Had she thrown it away or just held it so loosely
that the wind had caught it before she had fastened it?

"Oh, Mummy," Susy shrieked. "Oh, Mummy,
please stop the car, we've lost something."

Mummy started slowing down, but Ellen shook her
head as they all looked back. "No use," she said. "It
went right into that brook we were crossing."

Now Susy's lip curved more than ever. "Two
spoiled," she said. "Two lovely surprises. One's all
gone and the other's too big!" Her big blue eyes were
afloat with tears.

Jeff just couldn't stand that. "Listen," he said suddenly. "My surprise isn't spoiled. Even if it's too big for Blackie it isn't too big for me. If Blackie can't wear it in the show, I can wear it while I'm showing him. It'll be a sort of—of—exhibitor's badge."

Susy gave a little snort of surprise and started smiling, with the tears still rolling down her face. "Oh, Jeff," she said. "Oh, Jeff, isn't that lucky?"

Jeff forced himself to grin, but he didn't think it was lucky. And by the time he got to the show grounds, he was sure it wasn't lucky at all.

The show grounds covered the whole of the Stewart's huge open lawn. There were pets everywhere and most of them good, expensive, respectable-looking pets. There was a big Irish wolfhound, a whole cat club of cats, several ponies, and even Timmy Anderson's little brown donkey. Jeff began to feel it was pretty silly showing a crow, let alone showing a crow

when you had the better part of an ashcan strung around your neck.

Jeff wished the special pet class would never come. But like all the things you want to put off, it came especially quickly. The dog class was over, the pony class was over, and then the chicken class was over. Ellen came out with a large ribbon around Emir's neck at the end of the cat class. Jeff wished that Susy could have won it, but when he saw her face he knew she didn't care. She looked round and cheerful and just bursting with pride.

"Oh, Jeff," she said. "I do want to see you and Blackie all dressed up."

Somewhere, way deep inside of him, Jeff sighed, but he put the hodge-podge of tin and cardboard around his neck and tried to grin. "All dressed up like a crazy man," he thought to himself and wished that he could suddenly disappear.

When Jeff got into the ring, he wished so more than ever. There was a pet pig, a goat, two lambs, one tame hawk, and a pigeon. They were all queer pets, but a lame crow was the queerest, especially when the lame crow's owner made a jangly noise with every step he took.

"Oh, look at Jeff!" some of the children shouted.
"All tricked out like a scrap basket! Oh, look, oh,
look!"

Even Blackie gave a nervous little flutter on Jeff's shoulder at the sudden noise. For a moment Jeff thought Blackie might fly away and thus save him the agony of the rest of the show, but no such luck! Blackie gave one little shake and nestled down closer than ever to Jeff's neck.

Mr. Stewart was standing in the middle of the ring reading the rules of the class. "This exhibition of very special and unusual pets is to be judged on three counts: the health of the pet, the obedience of the pet, and his devotion to his owner."

Mrs. Hamersby, who was the other judge, nodded so that the imitation cherries and plums on her hat made little knocking noises against each other.

"The first prize is three dollars," Mr. Stewart went on. "The second——"

Jeff never even listened about the prizes. He didn't have a chance to begin with, and with Mrs. Hamersby as the judge he didn't have even the chance of a

chance. Mrs. Hamersby would remember how Blackie had spoiled her cake at the Sunday School picnic.

Each contestant in the "special pets" class had to bring his pet to the center of the lawn. For the first time Jeff wasn't ashamed. Blackie was still lame and always would be, but, except for that, two months had worked wonders. Blackie looked sleek and fat and his black feathers had a deep purple sheen.

"Your crow looks in fine shape," Mr. Stewart said pleasantly. Jeff wished he could nod without making his fool necklace rattle.

"Now the obedience test," Mr. Stewart called. "Your pet must show obedience to the owner and obedience to a stranger."

Jeff had tried hard to teach Blackie to come at a certain whistle. Sometimes it worked but more often it didn't. This time it worked like a charm. Jeff had barely raised his head when Blackie came flapping back to him.

Obedience to a stranger was the next test. For this, the animals were divided between the judges and Blackie fell to Mrs. Hamersby.

"It's all over now," Jeff thought. But when Mrs. Hamersby leaned forward clucking and calling so that the decorations on her hat rattled, Blackie went straight to her shoulder.

"And now for the final test," said Mr. Stewart, "to show affection for the owner." He uncovered a piece of canvas that had been put out in the center of the lawn. On it were oats, corn, lettuce, worms, and every other sort of food a very special pet might want. Each owner had to set his pet down near the food he liked best and then walk away. At a given signal, each owner was to call his own pet.

When Jeff set Blackie down near the canvas, the crow headed straight for a big pile of cherries and Jeff was sure he'd lost. Cherries were Blackie's favorite food and Jeff was positive he would never come away.

"Now," said Mr. Stewart when all the animals were eating, "each owner will call in turn and we will time his pet's quickness in obeying."

First it was Timmy Anderson's turn. He called and called, but the burro never raised its head from the good oats. The boy with the lamb called next, and after

a long, long time the lamb came, dribbling corn from its mouth.

"He's won it," Jeff thought. "He's won and there's no point in my even trying." But of course when his turn came, he did try. He started right in clapping his hands to attract Blackie's attention. As he clapped, his necklace rattled and the very next moment Blackie darted forward, away from the cherries! He flapped and hustled and cuddled down on Jeff's shoulder, until some of that ridiculous shiny necklace was actually underneath him.

There was a sudden crackle of applause and in another minute every child at the show was shouting and cheering for Jeff and Blackie. Even Mr. Stewart clapped as he handed Jeff three dollars in crisp new bills.

"But it just happened," Jeff gulped, feeling sillier
than ever. "It's this cr-crazy necklace my kid sister
made. I didn't understand it myself until just now."

Mr. Stewart laughed, and Mrs. Hamersby laughed so that her hat clicked and Blackie cocked his head at her.

"It doesn't matter how it's done, Sonny," Mr. Stewart said. "The point is that crow's mighty smart."

Jeff couldn't say anything. He couldn't even say thank you, until he'd found Susy. "You ought to have won it," he said. "You made the decoration."